Old and New Friends

Casey Martin

WestBow Press books may be ordered through booksellers or by contacting:

WestBow Press
A Division of Thomas Nelson & Zondervan
1663 Liberty Drive
Bloomington, IN 47403
www.westbowpress.com
1 (866) 928-1240

Custom Illustration by Gennel Marie Sollano and coordinated by Joseph Ramsey.

ISBN: 978-1-9736-9701-5 (sc)
ISBN: 978-1-9736-9702-2 (e)

Library of Congress Control Number: 2020913186

Print information available on the last page.

WestBow Press rev. date: 7/31/2020

WESTBOW
PRESS®
A DIVISION OF THOMAS NELSON
& ZONDERVAN

To my daughter, Jane.

There once was a family who loved to entertain.

Hosting dinners, having parties, and sharing
play dates were a part of everyday life.

Their friends were many.

The most faithful friends were Happiness,
Comfort, Consistency, and Love.

One day the family suddenly experienced a great loss.

The dinners halted. The parties were no more and the play dates became a thing of the past.

By no fault of their own, most of their faithful friends stopped coming over. Happiness said it felt unwelcome. Comfort couldn't remember where they lived. Consistency claimed it never knew them.

But Love still visited often.

The family felt sad that their faithful friends had forgotten them, but they soon found new friends visiting. Grief, Fear, and Anger started to make regular appearances.

Grief was by far the most loyal friend, but was also the loneliest.

Fear often showed up unannounced and lurked in dark corners.

Anger was the most startling. It didn't come often, but it loved to surprise the family and cause chaos.

The new friends were different and would take getting used to, but at least they were around.

Love still visited the family often. In fact, Love became
more present when the new friends started coming
over. At first the family wondered if it was because
Love enjoyed the company of the new friends.

But then the tension between all of the friends
became obvious. The family felt overwhelmed.

Finally, when it felt like too much, the family decided it didn't want to be in charge of hosting friends anymore.

Could their oldest, most faithful friend, Love, take over the responsibility?

Love was delighted to help.

Love immediately
banished Fear.

Love told Anger that it
wasn't welcome anymore.

Grief was allowed to stay, but it couldn't be lonely.
Love was going to work with Grief.

Love started sending invitations to new friends. Faith, Hope, and Peace.

Faith was strong and had a spotless memory of Love.
Hope was sure and steady, much like Consistency but sweeter.
Peace was restful and often accompanied by another friend, Joy.

The family invited Love to move in with them. Love was responsible for opening the door to any guest.

Many friends were welcomed.

Some were not.

Loss changed the family forever,
but Love said it wasn't in vain.

The family trusted Love and the family was more thankful for Love than ever before.

And so we know and rely on the love God
has for us. God is love. Whoever lives in
love lives in God, and God in them.

1 John 4:16